For all the children on the autistic spectrum,
those who love them, and, of course, for Drew.

www.mascotbooks.com

For more information, please contact:
Mascot Books
620 Herndon Parkway, Suite 320
Herndon, VA 20170
info@mascotbooks.com

Library of Congress Control Number: 2020905980

CPSIA Code: PRT0620A
ISBN-13: 978-1-64543-494-8

Printed in the United States

This Is Drew

Catherine White

Illustrated by Inna Eckman

This is Drew. He has autism. Can you tell?

Probably not at first, but keep watching how he acts and listen to how he talks.

Maybe when you ask him a question, he doesn't answer it or even look at you.

How does that make you feel?

Probably confused, and you might think that he doesn't want to be your friend.

The truth is he *does* want to be your friend. He just doesn't understand that not answering your question might hurt your feelings.

Maybe one day, the teacher says to the class, "Okay everybody, time to go back to your seats," and everyone takes their seats except Drew.

Maybe you think he just doesn't want to go sit down in his chair, but it's more likely that he doesn't understand that the word "everybody" means him, too.

Maybe you see Drew get really upset and cry a lot about things that wouldn't upset you.

How does that make you feel?

Maybe a little frustrated because he's getting extra attention from the teacher.

Maybe even a little scared because his crying is so loud it hurts your ears.

He's probably crying because he can't think of the right words to tell the teacher what is bothering him.

Imagine what it's like for Drew...

not to understand how important it is to answer a friend's question,

or know the meaning of certain words,

or be able to find the words to tell someone what's upsetting him

when everyone else all around him can do these things.

Why is it so hard for Drew to talk and act like everyone else?

Autism makes Drew think differently from you. It's difficult for his brain to take in everything we

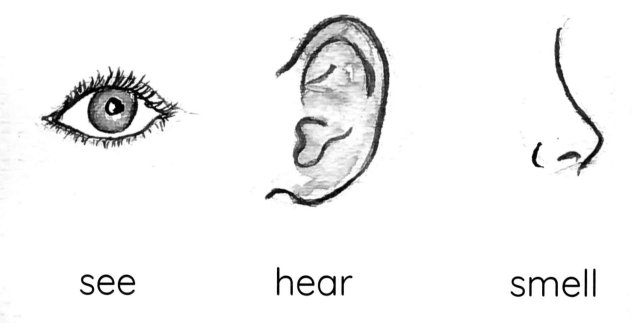

see   hear   smell

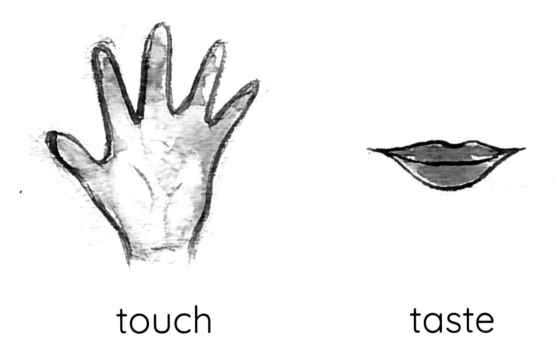

touch   taste

and put these five senses together like a
puzzle to understand the world around him.

Here's an example. What is happening in this picture?

You would probably say you see a boy at the beach who looks sad because it's about to storm so his mom is packing up their things.

Not only do you notice the boy, beach, and buckets, but also the lightning bolt and dark clouds, the mom leaving, and the sad look on the boy's face.

But when you ask Drew to look at the same picture, he might only see a boy at the beach building sandcastles.

He doesn't notice the mom packing up or the storm coming or how sad the boy looks,

and if he misses even one of these things, then he really doesn't understand what is happening in the picture.

While your brain lets you look at everything and put together a **whole** story, his brain only sees **pieces** of a story.

So, what can you do to help him?

You can ask your teacher what is the best way to be his friend.

Maybe they'll tell you to sit beside him at lunch or ask him to swing on the playground,

or maybe they will say just be kind and understanding and remember we are all different.

We all have our strengths and challenges, and the things we are not as good at we keep working to make better.

Maybe you're really good at making friends and following directions, but math is harder for you.

For Drew, it's the opposite.

He's really good at math, but it's not so easy for him to make friends or follow directions.

So be kind and realize that he's trying every day to be a better Drew,

just like you're trying every day to be a better you.

Comprehension Questions

- What are some ways that Drew is different from you?

- What are some ways that Drew is the same as you?

- Everyone has strengths and challenges. What did you notice in the story that were Drew's strengths? What were his challenges? What are some of your own strengths and challenges?

- Try this sensory exercise to imagine what every day might feel like for someone with autism:

  - Sit between two friends. Have them begin talking to you at the same time about something they are excited about for thirty seconds. When the thirty seconds are over, discuss what the experience was like for the person in the middle. Were you able to hear what each friend asked? How did you feel trying to understand both questions at the same time?

- Now that you know more about what it may be like to have autism, what are some ways you could be a good friend to someone like Drew who has autism?

About the Author

Catherine and her husband, Paul, have two children, Sarah and Drew, two dogs, Cricket and Pepper, and live near Washington, D.C. Catherine has served on the advisory committee for students with disabilities for her local school board, where she advocates for Drew and other children with disabilities.

About the Illustrator

Inna Eckman is a watercolor specialist who in 2014 started her illustration business, ArtAccent Illustrations, in the Charlotte, North Carolina area. She is the mother of three boys and is passionate about family, children, and art.

A Note from the Author

While the examples given in *This Is Drew* may not exactly mirror a child with autism that you personally know, it is important to note, as the experts on autism tell us, that what all children with autism have in common are challenges with communication, social skills, and repetitive behaviors. It is just a matter of degree. They can display mild, moderate, or severe behaviors in these areas. But regardless of degree, children with autism deserve our understanding and respect.

The real Drew with his cousin, Claire